THE ZOMBIE HIGHWAY

G. O. Clark

Illustrated by
Marge Simon

DARK REGIONS PRESS
– 2018 –

Dark Regions Press, LLC.
500 Westover Drive #12565
Sanford, NC 27330
United States of America

www.darkregions.com

Third Trade Paperback Edition
ISBN-10: 1-72584-980-8
ISBN-13: 978-1-72584-980-1

Contents

SCENES ALONG
THE ZOMBIE HIGHWAY

At the Tipping Point

You're in a cheap cafe,
eating the breakfast special, sipping
watered down coffee, when you
notice the guy at the far end
of the counter.

He looks old, but seems
young; hair uncombed, skin
a sickly gray, dark suit looking
slept in, both hands shakily raising
a coffee cup to his lips.

You think, poor guy,
tossed out on the street by his
wife, on the edge of losing his job,
likely spent the night on a park bench,
just trying to get by.

Eating your greasy-spoon fare,
you wonder if you should start up
a conversation with him, give an ear
to his verbal blues; two guys
just trying to survive.

Before you can follow through,
he lunges over the counter at the poor
waitress, bends her over his untouched
breakfast, and starts gnawing on her
face, biting deeper and deeper

as if trying to get inside
her skull to feast on her brains,
scrambled eggs no longer appetizing.
In time the big picture will come into
focus, the consequences of the

incurable, mutated virus become
old news. On this singular morning,
however, you're ringside at the tipping
point, the end of the status quo,
the rise of the living dead.

Little Zombies

It's Halloween night
and all the little zombies
are stumbling from house to house,
pressing doorbells with rotting fingers,
gurgling trick or treat, trick or treat
through yellowed, broken teeth,
bloody bags thrust forward for candy,
pennies and that all time favorite,
slow witted human brains,
the adults handing out the goodies
so amused by the cute little zombies
that they never see the trick coming,
each about to become the bloody treat.

The Carolers

The zombie carolers
crowd my front doorstep,
their voices slurred,
badly mangling "Jingle Bells,"
the beginning of each chorus
sounding like *jellied brains,*
jellied brains, need some
right away, while spastically
flailing their arms around and
clumsily marching in place
like decaying wooden soldiers.

New Moon/No Pulse

It's the new moon,
and the zombies are sluggish,
milling around on street corners,
stumbling about the cemetery,
wandering aimlessly in the night
in search of fleshy leftovers,

allowing even the weakest human
to dance circles around them,
beneath the star-bright sky,
the cycle of the heavens like
a ticking clock, the silence inside
each zombie's head complete.

The Picnic Is Over

A perfect summer's
day for a simple picnic lunch,
in the solitude of the city cemetery,
away from all the hustle and
bustle of corporate life.

Skyscrapers look down
upon the peaceful afternoon,
giant, hollow cement and glass
tombstones now filled with
the bones of the living.

The mighty buildings
still stand tall, but lifeless.
The cemetery quietly waits,
its headstones toppled, flowers
trampled, graves empty.

Perfect summer days
have given way to endless nights
of flesh eating zombies picnicking
without pause, not even the graves
immune to the madness.

Seasons of the Living Dead

Come spring
the snow pack melts
and the zombies thaw out,
picking up where they left off
before the winter freeze.

Summertime
is hard on decaying bodies,
the strongest sunscreen no longer
an option, sunglasses useless,
swimwear a bloody joke.

In autumn
the leaves turn, days grow
shorter, nights cooler and the
living dead perform their gruesome
tricks for bloody treats.

Winter brings
huddled nights by the fire,
burnt out Christmas lights, off-key
zombie carolers in the distance, and an
empty toast to the New Year.

Saturday Night Social Scene

The uninvited dinner guests
feast upon their hosts and hostesses,
paté de cerveau most popular,

as music fills the ballroom,
animated corpses lurching about the
dance floor to a Strauss waltz.

Eventually one of them will
tip over a candle, set the mansion
ablaze, then, unwittingly led

by a couple of flaming
undead torches, they'll all wander
away into the night to another soiree,
and party like animals 'til sunrise.

Zombiemobile

The zombiemobile
has no gas, and three flat tires,

but keeps on thumping along.

The zombiemobile
is stuffed full of lurid bodies,

like a post-apocalyptic clown car.

Riding in the zombiemobile
is reserved for the most ruthless,

those pushing it a slavish mob.

The zombiemobile doesn't
stop for pedestrians, living or dead,

nobody cognizant behind the wheel.

The zombiemobile
mostly travels in random circles,

in the wake of its own fetid exhaust,

the crazed night of zombie cruising,
screeching to a halt come sunup.

Zombie Clowns

Zombie clowns
are the worst with their
bulbous red noses, floppy,
over-sized cartoon shoes,
mop-like orange hair
and baggy clothes.

Blood stained,
makeup smeared, tripping
over their own feet, mindlessly
miming forgotten things,
the dark street is their ring,
the night, ringmaster.

Players in your
walking dead nightmare,
they stand out like day-glow
balloons in a cemetery, pleasant
memories of circuses past
forgotten at first bite.

The Ventriloquist

He was the highlight
of every show,
a star of the cabarets
early in his career,
a great accompanying act
at the casinos
in his twilight years.

His dummy
was a miniature of himself.
Same green and yellow
plaid suit, red tie,
and NY Yankees baseball cap.
Even the same jet black hair,
receding on the ventriloquist
later in life.

Their dialog
was always topical.
Politicians, movie stars
and current events providing
the necessary raw material,
his hand animating its
wooden movements,
his voice its spirit.

Among the other
victims of the plague,
they alone stand out, wandering

the city streets in the ragged
remnants of their stage presence,
blankly muttering
and moaning to the smoky sky,
brainless dummies
in search of a live audience.

You Just Can't Get Good Help Anymore

The zombie carpenters
keep falling off the scaffolding,
kicking over the paint buckets,
and crucifying each other
with their nail guns.

They're no longer
following the blueprints,
or the demands of the foreman
who's head and body now reside
on opposite sides of town.

Their constructions
are surreal, no two houses alike,
the carpenter's level unused,
2x4 framework a twisted nightmare
like the carpenters themselves.

Slapstick

The zombie police are
like a squad of Keystone Cops
mindlessly performing their slapstick
routines for a dwindling audience.

Unlike their silent movie
predecessors, their bloody antics
move in slow motion, yet each and all
survive the pratfalls unscathed.

In place of night sticks,
they use the bones of their victims
to crack open the skulls of the living,
eager for warm brains.

Their official police van is a
burnt out hulk, their uniforms filthy rags,
and blood curdling screams now take
the place of audience laughter.

Pool Party

It's summer,
thermometer pushing 90,
and the zombies have taken
over the hotel's kidney shaped
swimming pool.

Some are haphazardly
reclining on poolside chaise
lounges, gnawing on leftover pieces
of the not-so-lucky hotel guests,
soaking up the moon-rays.

Others are spastically
enjoying the pool, rotting skin
flakes left in their wakes, one fat
fellow doing belly flops over and over
into the shallow end, yelling out
what sounds like *Geronimo*.

From a distance
it seems an inviting scene
to any hot, tired travelers passing
by on the highway. Close up, though,
its just another unintentional trap
for the unwary.

Night Parade

After sunset,
the zombie parade
forms ranks,

ineptly marches
up the avenue, step
by deadly step,

band music
replaced by guttural
grunts and groans;

fire engines, floats,
antique cars gathering
dust elsewhere,

parade gaiting
horses gone the way
of all flesh,

the zombies
marching on for blood,
brains and anarchy.

Zombie on a Leash

Like a stiff legged dog
on a leash

she's yanked this way
and that,

a post-mortem slave of
circumstance

bound to her master, her
pimp,

a decaying pleasure doll
sold into the

cold embrace of some
faceless necrophiliac.

Zombie Loner

He stands alone,
ragged and bent,
separate from the pack,
even in death
belonging nowhere.

The traditional
zombies, victims
of the voodoo curse,
are cliquish,
not open to new members.

The radioactive,
alien infested zombies –
hostages to the invisible –
have no say
as to who gets an invite.

The plague victim
zombies don't care who
rots with them, but his
immune system is too strong,
even though dead.

So he stumbles
through death alone,
feared by those still living,
ostracized by the dead,
odd man out
in a world gone mad.

Scarecrow

Its brain
is made of straw,
its clothes torn, dirty rags
loosely hung upon a
rib-less body,

its eyes,
empty sockets,
its mouth stitched closed,
and its nonsectarian crucifixion
a cobbled together affair

witnessed
by a zombie priest,
kneeling in the corn field,
clerical collar speckled with blood,
gazing ever heavenward.

Writer's Block

Staring at
the blank sheet of white
typing paper poking out of the
old Olympics' platen,

he doesn't have a clue
what to do, how to do it, or why,
terrible hunger pains all he
can think about.

Being a famous writer has
lost all its glamour since becoming
one of them; body rotting away,
fans a mindless mob.

The critics no longer exist.
Deadlines are a thing of the past.
And the major literary award he won,
now serves as a bludgeon.

Roadside Shrines

Nobody knows why
roadside shrines attract the
walking dead, distracting them
from their bloody trek.

Composed of simple
wooden crosses, votive candles,
plastic flowers and stuffed toys,
these simple offerings to an
absentee god along the deadliest
stretches of lonesome highway,
stop them cold in their
mindless tracks.

They pause and
blankly stare at the shrines,
perhaps just trying to remember
what it was like to be human,
soulless moans escaping
their twisted mouths, one or two
even reaching down to touch
a teddy bear or plastic rose.

Those who hunt the
walking dead – axes sharp,
shot guns cocked – know a golden
opportunity when they see one.

The Library

Books litter the floor.
CDs, DVDs and video tapes
have toppled from their racks.
Public computers lay smashed
in their corrals. The library
has been abandoned by
its everyday patrons.

It was once a refuge
for the bookish. A safe
place for after school study.
A depository of facts for those
seeking advice from Consumer
Reports, S&P Indexes, and,
a retreat for the homeless.

Now it serves as a
dormitory of sorts for the
living dead, who huddle far
back in the book stacks, hiding
from the sun, waiting for the
fall of night to continue their
nocturnal mayhem.

Sometimes one of them
will pick up a fallen tome,
turn it over in its rotting hands,
even chew on a papery edge, then
toss it aside with a grunt, wrong

kind of nourishment,
bloodless pulp.

The living no longer have
time for books, post-apocalyptic
survival taking up all their free time,
that same free time in recent years
spent on TV, movies, Internet,
and video games. The books
gone to dust.

Zombies Crossing

The road sign
warns in large black letters,
ZOMBIES CROSSING,
here along Highway 49
deep in the Sierra foothills.

Rusty and bullet riddled,
it's become obsolete,
the living dead truly dead now,
Nature once again cleaning up
another human mess.

The sign was
originally a joke,
cobbled together at the
local fender bender shop,
a half serious warning to any
motorist fleeing the cities;
there's zombies in these here hills,
best keep movin' along.

At the time
of the sign's installation,
the hills were still free of the
living dead; television-distant,
townsfolk complacent.
Things changed.

Of course most
drivers glimpse road signs
peripherally as high speed blurs,
which proved beneficial to the town's
new demographic, human brains
preferred over those of deer.

The sign still states
in faded black letters,
ZOMBIES CROSSING,
though there's nobody left alive
to heed its warning.

Road Kill

The one-legged
zombie trucker mindlessly
tooling along in his 18 wheeler,
ignores the English accented,
female voice of the GPS,
brakes a forgotten concept,
pedal to the metal,
always veers towards hitchhikers —
evidenced by the truck's bumper and grill —
as he heads for destinations unknown,
abandoned truck stops but a blur
in the semi's cracked rearview mirror.

Albino

The albino zombie
finds that fresh blood
adds rouge to his cheeks,
and no longer feels like
an outsider, accepted as is
by his fellow living dead.

It doesn't matter
that the same folks who
once considered him a freak
are now bent on chopping off
his pink eyed, white haired,
deathly pale head.

He's all zombie now,
dead to the behind-his-back
whisperings of strangers
and friends alike, done with
the old pretenses of society,
the past a total blank.

Rag Doll

Little Jill
got left behind with
nothing but the clothes on
her back, and a rag doll.

Now little Jill
blindly wanders the
streets and back alleys, totally
lost, and forgetful.

Little Jill has been
shot twice, run over by a car,
and fallen off a bridge, but still
keeps shuffling along.

The 2012 Pandemic
stole little Jill's childhood,
wiped her mind clean of cartoons
and ice cream dreams.

Little Jill imitates
the mindless actions of her elders,
following the pack from one
fresh kill to another.

Poor little Jill, bloody
rag doll clutched in her tiny
dead hand, warm blood replacing
Kool-Aid as her favorite drink.

Clothes Make the Zombie

Who says zombies all
look alike, ragged, and bloody.

Here's one wearing a
black tuxedo and wing-tip shoes,

the prom turned *Carrie* in the end.

How about the one in scrubs,
blood stained from work, or worse,

operating room abandoned to the rats.

Or the professional business woman,
dressed in her gray pants-suit,

fresh from some board-room slaughter.

Here's a housewife, in a calico dress,
shambling along to the market,

hubby and kids decaying back home.

Policemen, mechanics, coeds
and joggers, all dressed in character,
this post-apocalyptic world their stage.

A Stop along the Post-Apocalyptic Tour

The cuckoo clock
has turned quite sinister
in the darkened parlor
of your ancestors,

that very same room
where ornately framed
your nightmares linger atop
a keyless piano.

Outside, the lunatic
parade flows around the
tinted windows of an idling
black stretch limo,

chauffeur asleep at the
wheel, white as piano keys,
stiff as a wooden bird's beak,
silent as a 4 AM closet.

When the clock
cuckoos your cue, and the
impatient horn begs departure,
you bag up your scars,

exchange bony hugs
all around, and slip out into
the zombie night, next gig,
the gallows stage.

The Curse of the Aware Zombie

He was labeled a zombie
when the ER nurse found no pulse.

He considered he was a zombie
when his suit hung on him like bloody rags.

He surmised he was a zombie
when he no longer feared getting a sunburn.

He decided he was a zombie
when his picking of one's brain turned literal.

He understood he was a zombie
when the hunters kept aiming for his head.

He realized he was a zombie
when his reality became stranger than fiction.

He accepted the fact he was a zombie
just before his thoughts turned to mush.

Zombie Eyes

The zombie's eyes,
they show no sign of life,
their souls sliced out with
a voodoo knife.

Dressed in old rags,
never breaking a sweat,
their night on the town
makes death a sure bet.

They fall into step
at the Master's command,
mindless, evil minions
wreaking havoc on demand.

Their favorite cuisine,
the warm flesh of the living,
their restaurant of choice,
a town most unforgiving.

The zombie's eyes,
they show no sign of life,
their souls sliced out
by the Master's knife.

Reanimated

Cartoon zombies
have taken over the
towns and cities of the
real world.

Betty Boop
stumbles along like
a bloody bobble head,
spring all but shot.

Mickey and Minnie
fight over the remains
of Pluto, ripping at his flesh
like starving hyenas.

Bugs Bunny
gnaws on Elmer Fudd's
dismembered arm as if it
were a fresh carrot.

Rocky and Bullwinkle
work as a team; moose
cornering the meat, squirrel
dive-bombing the brains.

The Flintstones,
Jetsons, Simpsons and
the Family Guy's brood,
all real as Roger Rabbit,

reanimated by some
deity's twisted sense of humor,
the end of the world a crazed
Looney Tune nightmare.

Some Things Zombies Suck At

Conga lines and line dancing.
Juggling and tight-rope walking.
Throwing fondue parties.
Eating candied apples.
Texting, and texting while driving.
Public speaking of any kind.
Giving massages.
Barbering, or hair styling.
Carving Jack-O-Lanterns.
Decorating Christmas trees.

Some Advice to Prospective Zombies

Zombies should
never attempt karaoke,
or one-liners.

This should be a
no-brainer, but after dining
they tend to lose all
inhibition.

Letting them
dance at wedding receptions
isn't recommended.

They're all left feet
and personal hygiene deficient,
thus real spoilers of pastel
colored chiffon's.

Really sore losers that
they are, they've been banned
from all TV game shows.

Being slowwitted and
clumsy just doesn't cut it in the
fast paced world of buzzer
activated trivia.

Zombies should stick
to what they've always been
the most proficient at,

scaring the bejesus
out of the living, a rare kind
of talent that comes naturally
to the walking dead.

Breaking News

The local news crew
filming the outbreak live,
unwittingly become victims
of their own reporting, a snarling
group of the walking dead
surrounding them,

their first hand broadcast
streaming live into millions
of households, stunned viewers
watching in horror as the carnage
unfolds, the DTV images
blurring to red,

the surround sound
screams bombarding the
senses, the real world fast becoming
a sordid reality that no amount
of channel surfing will
ever change.

Playtime's Over

She used to see
teddy bears, unicorns
and kitty cats in the clouds.
Now she just sees
dead people.

She once believed
there was a monster under
her bed. Now she hides
there each night from
the horror beyond her door.

She remembers
when nightmares were
forgotten upon waking, after
her mother's hug. Now
she fears sleep.

She wonders
when her parents will
return home, her dog stop
whimpering, and the moaning
outside go away.

She prays that her
guardian angel appears
and flies her up to the clouds
she once loved, before the dead
came out to play.

Two Drink Minimum

The zombie audience
mimics the motions of the
living, their dead eyes reflecting
the flickering candles
upon the tables,

as the dark haired,
rose lipped cabaret singer,
bathed by a blood red spotlight,
performs her world weary,
sultry song,

playing to those
long forgotten impulses,
mutated dreams, and impotent
Viagra blues of the
living dead,

this final night
of the human species
spreading across the dying Earth
like a long, drawn out,
toxic breath.

Bottom of the Ninth

It stands there
bloodied and gaunt,
a human tibia clutched
in its right hand, pointed
towards the stands,

somewhere in its
brain the dying memory
of The Babe, two generations
removed, his iconic stance
and superstar nerve

playing out now
in a packed stadium,
on zombie time, the roar
of the crowd replaced by the
screams of the living,

the human race
in its final inning, the
thing at the plate waiting
for a pitch in its wheelhouse,
spitting out a wad of brain.

Old Flame

Found her in rags
wandering the zombie highway
a while back, blue eyes glazed over,
lips stained red from a bloody kiss,
her latest one night stand forgotten
before it even started.

That high school yearbook
photo never did her real justice;
the natural beauty, optimistic take
on life, and ability to light up the dark
corners of my adolescent world
with feather-sharp clarity.

I was wrong to let her
leave that night, my unwillingness
to commit the final straw, the evidence
on TV of the escalating carnage outside,
no deterrent to a broken heart,
the echo of hers still haunting me.

Dead Eyes in a Rearview Mirror

Heading home late, a lone,
crazed semi trucker has me pinned
in his high beams, eighteen wheeler hissing
along the tarmac, stalking this rural interstate,
hot orange running lights in the form of a cross
adorning the truck's radiator, blazing
in my rearview mirror.

Other truckers are parked
and sleeping peacefully along the roadside,
unaware of the deadly scenario playing out nearby,
running lights marking their rest like Christmas lights
along roof eaves, snug in their bunks dreaming
of flesh toned curves, and strong, black coffee.

It's just me and this maniac
careening through the dark silence,
a lone zombie trucker Hell bent on crucifying me in
some unborn-again way, cold steel against warm flesh,
screeching tire choir testifying in the still night,
my final destination tied to the muddled
actions of the living dead.

Road Trip Advice

The trip down
this zombie highway
is the only avenue of escape,
your wife's minivan stuffed full,
the territory ahead a truly
Hellish landscape.

The trip down
this zombie highway
is not recommended for the kids;
pop in a Disney DVD to distract them,
the reality beyond their windows
a bloody mess.

The trip down
this zombie highway
will surely give you nightmares,
so concentrate on the road ahead,
and never stop to lend a helping hand
or set out flares.

The trip down
this zombie highway
could well be your family's last.
Steel your heart against the dark future,
leave the burning cities behind,
don't dwell on the past.

All In the Family

His mom and dad
never told him about their
alien abductions.

His sister never shared
her stories about being part of a
college vampire clique,

and his brother
kept silent about his wartime
run-ins with zombies.

He learned these facts
later from his bohemian uncle,
the family artiste,

their keeper of secrets,
who one night over steak and ale
divulged quite a few,

including a most startling one,
which convinced him to become a
vegan, and avoid a full moon.

Some Zombies One Should Avoid

Zombie politicians –
who linger over your brain,
take forever to finish their task,
then shake your limp hand in the end.

Salesmen zombies –
who push their mindless sales pitch
upon you, crowding your front door and
trashing your living room carpet if
given the chance.

Evangelical zombies –
who act blankly determined to
save your soul, to convert you to their
fuzzy belief systems and twisted visions
of eternity.

Radio talk show zombies –
who babble on throughout the night
to their half-conscious listeners, the later
willfully offering up their gray matter
to irrational half truths.

Corporate zombies –
who march around in expensive,
but tattered business suits, flailing their
MBA's in your face, determined to drag
you down to their bottom line.

Finally, zombie relatives –
those you haven't seen for years,
those who repeatedly sponge off you,
and those who literally interpret the proverb,
blood is thicker than water, intent on
draining you of every last drop.

Quotes from the Zombie Fact Book

"Zombies love television,
but are totally inept when it
comes to using the remote
control."

"At drive-in movies
they stumble around from
car to car unable to remember
where they parked."

"Miniature golf to zombies
is like a maze filled with once
familiar landmarks from a past
they can't remember."

"The musical ring tones
of their cell phones makes them
walk around in circles trying
to locate the sound."

"Well behaved zombies
are always welcome at political
rallies, church services, and
golf tournaments."

"Zombies are easy
targets, like shooting gallery
ducks, going round and round,
always returning for more."

"They make good extras
in zombie movies, already dressed
for the part, and emphatic when
delivering their lines."

"The humans in zombie
movies are usually just trying
to survive, while the zombies are
just trying to decompose."

"The walking dead
take themselves too seriously,
don't get punch lines, and never laugh
at their own pratfalls."

"Everything you thought
you knew about zombies, is never
quite enough, when the future comes
pounding at your door."

The Last Zombie

The last zombie on Earth
doesn't feel alone,
has no concept of its isolation,
pines for no one.

It still has a relentless appetite
for fresh brains,
but the competition is zilch
since becoming the last zombie.

In the abandoned, silent city
the last zombie stumbles
into nothing living or dead, not even
a stray cat or dog.

The last zombie will eventually
get hunted down,
a bullet to the head, or fire axe to its
muddled brain.

The survivors of the plague
will eventually spread tall tales about
the last zombie on Earth,
twisting the facts about its lineage.

G. O. Clark's writing has been published in *Asimov's Science Fiction, Analog, Talebones Magazine, Strange Horizons, Space & Time, Retro Spec: Tales of Fantasy and Nostalgia, A Sea Of Alone: Poems For Alfred Hitchcock, Tales Of The Talisman*, and many other publications. He's the author of ten poetry collections, the two most recent, *White Shift*, 2012, Sam's Dot Publishing, and, *Shroud of Night*, 2011, Dark Regions Press. His fiction collection, *The Saucer Under My Bed & Other Stories*, was published by Sam's Dot Publishing in 2011. He won the *Asimov's* Readers Award for poetry in 2001, and has been a repeat Rhysling and Bram Stoker Award® Nominee. He's retired, and lives in Davis, CA. Visit his website at http://goclarkpoet.weebly.com/.

Marge Simon's writing and art appear in publications such *as Strange Horizons, Niteblade, Daily SF Magazine, Pedestal Magazine, Dreams & Nightmares*. She edits a column for the *HWA Newsletter* and serves as Chair of the HWA Board of Trustees. Her poetry has won the *Strange Horizons* Readers Choice Award, the Bram Stoker Award®, the Rhysling Award and the Dwarf Stars Award. Collections include: *Like Birds in the Rain, Unearthly Delights, The Mad Hattery, Vampires, Zombies & Wanton Souls*, and *Dangerous Dreams*. Visit her website at www.margesimon.com.

Made in the USA
Columbia, SC
18 June 2024